WRITTEN BY **ED FREILER**
ILLUSTRATED BY **JEFF PAGAY**

Published and distributed by

ISLAND HERITAGE
P U B L I S H I N G
A DIVISION OF THE MADDEN CORPORATION

99-880 IWAENA STREET, AIEA, HAWAII 96701-3202
PHONE: (808) 487-7299 • FAX: (808) 488-2279
E-MAIL: HAWAII4U @ PIXI.COM

ISBN #0-89610-291-2

First Edition, Fourth Printing —1999

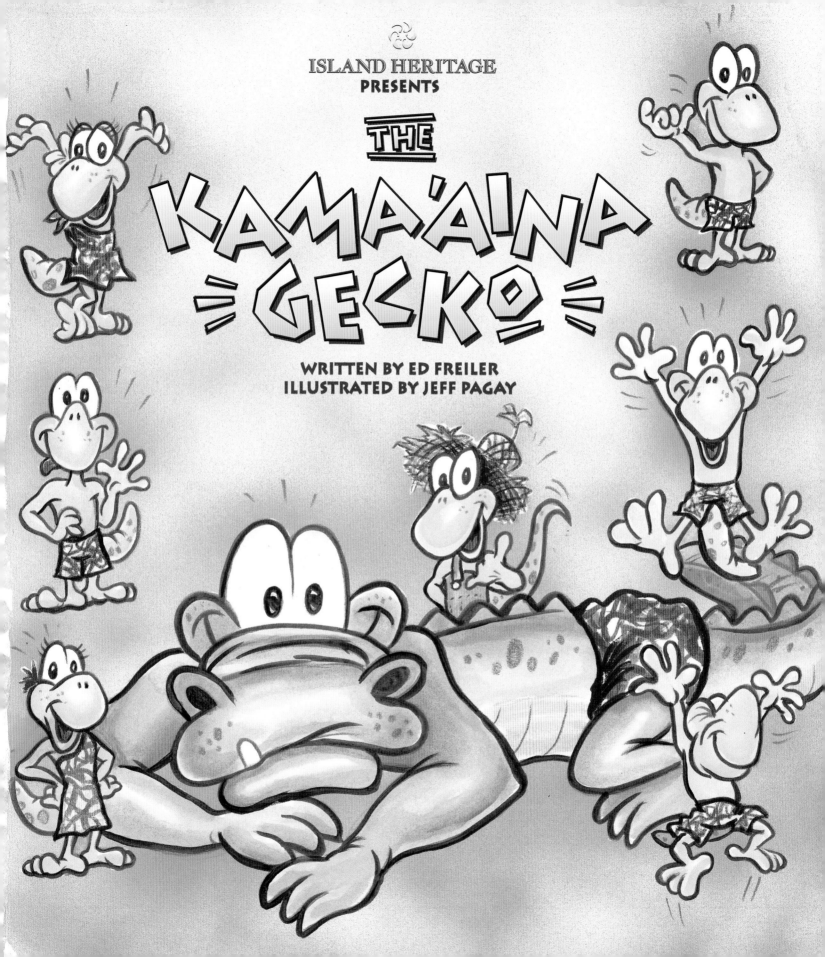

The zoo keeper watched as the big plane landed at Honolulu International Airport with a very special cargo. The box marked "HONOLULU ZOO - BE CAREFUL" was handed to the zoo keeper.

The cargo attendant laughed, "That is such a small box. What do you have in there?" he asked the zoo keeper. "Wild geckos?"

The zoo keeper smiled, "You can call them kama'aina geckos," and he untied the string around the box.

"Look," said the zoo keeper as he pointed to seven eggs. "They are perfect eggs! Mahalo for taking good care of them."

He was so excited about the new babies that
the zoo keeper forgot to close the box tight. He
put the box into the back of his truck
and drove onto the highway
leaving the airport behind.

As the truck went down the highway, **BOOM**...it hit a bump! Out of the box flew one egg, high into the sky. It will smash, yes indeed, when it hits the ground!

Down fell the egg and then, all of the sudden, it landed in the back of a big truck filled high with dirt.

The egg did not smash. The big truck turned off the highway and headed over the Pali.

The zoo keeper drove on to the zoo, not knowing he had lost an egg.

Heading up the Pali Highway, the truck went faster and faster. The wind blew dirt onto the road.

HONOLULU ZOO

8

WHOOSH, the wind picked up the egg and over the side of the road it went. The egg will get lost, yes indeed, in the underbrush and tangles of trees below!

The egg bounced on the leaves of a banana tree, then gently fell onto a taro plant. It slid down to a soft nest next to a stream. Inside the nest were six small eggs . . . and the new big egg. This made seven eggs in the nest.

The sun was bright and shone onto the eggs. One by one, the eggs cracked open as the new babies were hatched. One gecko, two geckos, three geckos, four geckos, five geckos, six geckos, and at last, number seven.

Number seven was much bigger and looked different from the geckos. **He was a baby alligator!**

An older gecko in a bush above the babies welcomed the new ones. "Aloha! Welcome to Ginger Falls Valley. I am Uncle Alakai. We are all family, an ohana of cousins."

Suwanna, the smallest gecko, screamed with delight, "This place is so pretty! Hello, my cousins."

Owen, a chubby little gecko stated, "I feel funny in my tummy."

Uncle Alakai laughed, "You are hungry and must learn to catch food."

"What do we eat?" asked Miki.

"The most delicious food in the world—BUGS!" shouted Uncle Alakai. "You must climb into the bushes and trees. There are plenty of bugs for all."

They all started to climb and it was fun. The big one, Eke, could not climb up the bushes and trees. The bushes just fell over. All the baby geckos laughed, except Suwanna.

She tried to help her bigger cousin and told him, "Eke, find a bigger tree to climb."

"I am not a very good tree climber, Uncle Alakai," said Eke, "but I am hungry, too!"

"Go into the water and you will find good food for you to eat, Eke," said Uncle Alakai. "You are a kama'aina gecko, and come from a far away place. You are our cousin just the same." Uncle Alakai knew that Eke was a baby alligator from the mainland. Eke went into the water and it was fun! Eke found lots of fish to eat. He paddled all around the swimming hole and was a very good swimmer.

Uncle Alakai warned the little geckos, "Do not go into the water until you learn to swim! It is very dangerous!"

Days went by and everybody got bigger. Eke got **much bigger**! All the cousins were afraid of Eke, except Suwanna. She loved her kama'aina cousin the same as all her cousins. Eke loved all his cousins too, even if they laughed at him for not being able to climb trees.

Owen yelled from high up in a tree, "You cannot climb this tree, the whole world you cannot see." Everyone laughed except Suwanna.

"Don't listen to him," Suwanna said, "He cannot swim and is jealous."

"I wish my other cousins would play with me. I could teach them all how to swim," said Eke.

During the day, Eke lay in the sun. It felt so good on his big back. Sometimes Suwanna slept on his big back, too. When Eke paddled around the swimming hole, Suwanna rode with him and it was so much fun. He taught her to swim, safely watching out for her.

One day the rain came down very hard. All the smaller cousin geckos hid under a bush to keep from getting wet. Eke tried to climb under the bush, too, but he crushed it. Owen yelled, "Eke, go away! We are getting wet!" "Go away, Eke!" said the other cousins, too!

Suwanna called softly to Eke, "Don't listen to them. Stay with us."

"They are right. I am getting them wet. I like the water, anyway." replied Eke, and he went to the waterfall to rest. The water from the falls felt good on his back.

The rain stopped and out came the sun with the most beautiful rainbow in Hawaii.

"I am going to touch the rainbow!" said Owen as he started to climb a tree.

"Be careful," cautioned Miki, "The tree is wet and slippery. I don't want you to fall."

"I am the best climber in Ginger Falls Valley and I am not afraid!" yelled Owen.

Away he went . . . up and up, higher and higher.

"Please, someone find Uncle Alakai! He must be told about Owen!" yelled Suwanna.

"Owen will be mad at you for telling Uncle Alakai," said Miki.
The other cousin geckos nodded their heads, agreeing with Miki.

"I will find Uncle Alakai! I do not care if Owen is mad at me. I love him and want him to be safe," yelled Suwanna as she ran into the forest to find Uncle Alakai.

"I can almost touch the rainbow!" yelled Owen from high up in the tree. "I just need to climb out on the very end of that branch."

His cousins looked up and watched him. Owen looked down and his cousins were very, very small. This was the highest Owen ever climbed. The branch he was on was over the swimming hole and he could see Eke near the waterfalls. Even Eke looked small to Owen!

"Look and see! I'm in the tree! Don't you wish that you were me!" yelled Owen to Eke.

Eke felt sad and hid under the water.

'I wish,' Eke thought, 'I wish I could climb trees, too!'

Miki yelled up, "Owen, please bring us all a piece of the rainbow! I want some of the **blue**."

All the cousins starting yelling.

"**Purple** for me!"

"I want a big piece of **red**!"

"Oh, the **orange** is so bright!"

CRACK

O wen was so proud that all the cousins
thought he was so brave. As he reached out to grab
some of the rainbow, he slipped on the wet bark. He
grabbed a smaller limb of the tree to keep from
falling. Owen held on and was okay.

CRACK!

The small tree limb broke and Owen started
falling down to the water below.

"HELP!" screamed Owen as he fell through the air.

SPLASH! went the water, and under went Owen.

"HELP HIM! HELP HIM! He cannot swim!" yelled Miki.
"Help!" yelled his cousins.

28

They could not help him because they could not swim. Suwanna and Uncle Alakai were not there to help Owen. The water turned calm and everybody was looking for Owen.

Miki started to cry. "We should have learned to swim!" She sniffed, "Now no one can save Owen!"

SWOOSH! **SPLASH!** The water started to make waves. All of a sudden, Owen rose up out of the water! He was on cousin Eke's big back! He was safe and okay! Quickly, Eke brought him onto the bank and Owen jumped off.

"Thank you for saving my life, cousin Eke," said Owen. He gave Eke a big gecko hug.

Miki and all the cousins cheered for Eke.

Suwanna and Uncle Alakai arrived and were happy that all the cousins loved each other very much.

Uncle Alakai said, "Just because you look different, Eke, does not mean we love you any different."

"I want you to teach me to swim! Please, cousin Eke!" begged Owen.
Before Eke could answer, all the cousins yelled, "Please, please! Us, too!"

Without saying anything, Eke turned away
from his cousins and walked to the water's edge.
He stopped and turned his head to look back
at his cousins.

With a big smile, Eke yelled, "**Jump on! Swimming lessons for everyone!**"

All the cousins jumped on Eke's big back and he paddled around the swimming hole. He was the happiest Kama'aina Gecko in the State of Hawaii.

THE END